POKÉMON™

Theme Song

I want to be the very best,
Like no one ever was.
To catch them is my real test,
To train them is my cause.
I will travel across the land,
Searching far and wide.
Each Pokémon, to understand
The power that's inside
Pokémon
(Gotta catch 'em all)
It's you and me
I know it's my destiny
Pokémon!
You're my best friend
In a world we must defend .
Pokémon
(Gotta catch 'em all)
A heart so true
Our courage will pull us through
You teach me and I'll teach you
Pokémon
(Gotta catch 'em all)
Gotta catch 'em all
Pokémon

Pokémon Theme
Words and Music by Tamara Loeffler and John Siegler
Copyright © 1998 Pikachu Music (BMI)
Worldwide rights for Pikachu Music administered by Cherry River Music Co. (BMI)
All Rights Reserved   Used By Permission

There are more books
about Pokémon.

Collect them all!

POKéMON™

Night in the Haunted Tower

Adapted by Tracey West

SCHOLASTIC INC.

New York   Toronto   London   Auckland   Sydney
Mexico City   New Delhi   Hong Kong

No part of this publication may be reproduced in whole or in part, or stored in a retrieval system, or transmitted in any form or by any means, electronic, mechanical, photocopying, recording, or otherwise, without written permission of the publisher. For information regarding permissions, write to Scholastic Inc., Attention: Permissions Department, 555 Broadway, New York, NY 10012.

ISBN 0-439-13742-X

12 11 10 9 8 7 6   9/9 0 1 2 3 4/0

Printed in the U.S.A.

First Scholastic printing, October 1999

The World of Pokémon

ndigo
lateau

Viridian
Forest

Pewter
City

Mt. Moon

Celadon
City

Cerulean
City

Sea
Cottage

Saffron
City

Viridian
City

Pallet
Town

Cinnabar
Island

Seafoam
Islands

Fuchsia
City

Vermilion
City

Lavender
Town

The Warp Tile

"I can't believe we finally made it to Saffron City!"

Ash Ketchum looked out at the sparkling city below him. Tall buildings gleamed in the sunlight.

"I know what I'm going to do first!" Ash said.

Ash's friend Misty shook her head. "Let me guess," she said. "I bet you want to go to the Saffron City Gym . . ."

". . . and battle the Gym Leader so you

can get a Marsh Badge," finished Ash's friend Brock.

"Of course!" Ash exclaimed. After all, that was what being a Pokémon trainer was all about. Ever since he turned ten, Ash had traveled far and wide, searching for Pokémon — creatures with amazing powers. To become a master Pokémon trainer, Ash would have to earn badges by battling his Pokémon against other Pokémon in the gym in each city. Then he could qualify to enter the Pokémon League Tournament. If he won that he would be a champion Pokémon trainer.

Now the three friends walked up to the gates of Saffron City.

Brock shook his head. "Sabrina is the Gym Leader in Saffron City. She fights with Psychic Pokémon. They're really hard to beat."

"Yeah, but she's never battled my Pikachu before," Ash said confidently. He picked up the small Pokémon at his feet.

"*Pika?*" asked Pikachu. The yellow Electric Pokémon with the lightning-shaped tail looked at Ash nervously.

Ash laughed. "Don't worry, Pikachu. You've helped me win so many battles already. I'm sure Sabrina's Psychic Pokémon will be a piece of cake."

"I guess we'll find out soon," Misty pointed out. "We're here!"

Ash looked up. Giant silver arches marked the entrance to Saffron City.

Suddenly, the sound of whistles and bells filled the night air. Two teenage girls appeared out of the darkness.

"You win! You win!" they cried.

"We what?" Ash was confused. The girls looked kind of strange. They both wore hula skirts and tropical shirts. One had long red hair, the other had shoulder-length purple hair.

"You're the one-millionth visitor to Saffron City," explained the redhead. She grabbed Ash's hand. "Follow us to get your grand prize!"

"Grand prize?" Ash exclaimed. "All right!" He followed the girls down the street.

Misty looked at Brock. "Something's fishy about this," she said. "We'd better go, too."

The girls led Ash, Pikachu, Misty, and Brock down the street to the Saffron City Hotel.

"After you," said the dark-haired girl.

The friends stepped through the door into a gleaming marble hallway.

Ash turned. "So where's the grand prize?" he asked.

The redhead smiled an evil smile. "You've won a trip — to the Warp Tile!"

Before Ash could react, the girl pushed him, Misty, and Brock into a room covered with large tiles. The dark-haired girl grabbed Pikachu and laughed.

4

"Hey!" Ash cried. The push sent him sprawling to the ground. Ash, Misty, and Brock landed on top of a tile in the middle of the room.

The tile began to shine with an orange glow.

"What's going —" Ash started to speak, but suddenly his voice froze. His body started to tingle. Ash looked at Brock and Misty. They were flickering, like an image on a movie screen. Then he looked down at *his* body. It was doing the same thing.

They were disappearing!

A split second later, Ash started to feel like himself again. He looked at his friends. They were back to normal. But something was different. They were in a new room.

The walls, floor, and ceiling of this room were covered with big, gray tiles. The tile they were on was still glowing orange.

"What's going on?" Ash asked, alarmed.

A giant TV screen slid down from the ceiling. The screen flicked on. The two teenage girls grinned at them.

"Prepare for trouble," they said gleefully, "and make it double!"

Ash stared as the girls took off their outfits to reveal two uniforms underneath. They weren't two teenage girls at all — they were Jessie and James, a pair of Pokémon thieves called Team Rocket!

Ash rose to his feet. "So it's *you!*" he yelled. "Get us out of here!"

"Sorry," Jessie said,

though she didn't sound sorry at all. "The Warp Tile is the only way in or out of the room."

"There's no way to escape!" James said, smiling.

"We've finally captured Pikachu!" said another voice.

It was Meowth, Team Rocket's talking, catlike Pokémon. And next to it was Pikachu — tied up with ropes!

"You better give Pikachu back right now!" Ash demanded.

"And get us out of here!" Misty shouted.

The screen went blank. Ash pounded on it with his fist.

"I've got to save Pikachu," Ash cried.

Brock looked thoughtful. "We've got to find a way out of here first. But we can't control the Warp Tile, and it's the only way in or out."

"Maybe not," Misty said. She pointed to a corner of the room.

A soft, blue ball of light had appeared in

the room. The friends watched in amazement as the blue light took shape.

It was a little girl. She was wearing a white dress. The brim of a large hat covered her face.

And she was carrying Pikachu!

"You rescued Pikachu!" Ash cried. "I don't know who you are, but thank you!"

The girl said nothing. Ash started to rush toward her, but he felt his body freeze. He couldn't move.

The blue light got brighter. Ash's body began to tingle. He saw Misty and Brock from the corner of his eye.

They were all disappearing again!

2

Abra vs. Pikachu

For a split second Ash could see nothing but flickering light. Then he saw Pikachu, Misty, and Brock appear in front of him. His body stopped tingling.

They had somehow been transported again. Ash looked around. Now they were in a gym unlike any he had ever seen before. The floor gleamed with cold marble. Tall, round pillars lined the walls. Lit candles sat on the pillars. A large platform stood at one end of the gym.

"Where are we?" Ash asked.

"I'm pretty sure it's the Saffron City Gym," Brock said.

"That's right."

Ash spun around at the sound of the spooky voice. A teenage girl was standing on the platform. Her icy blue eyes stared at them coldly. Her long, straight, dark hair nearly touched the ground.

"Sabrina!" Misty cried.

The Gym Leader didn't respond. A blue light began to glow from her hands. Ash watched in amazement as the little girl from the hotel appeared in Sabrina's arms. Only now Ash realized that it wasn't a little girl at all. It was a doll!

"You sent your doll to save Pikachu," Ash said. "You helped us. Why?"

Sabrina ignored him. "Would you like to have a match?"

Ash brightened. "A match? Of course! That's what we came here for. I need to earn my Marsh Badge."

Sabrina's eyes narrowed. "So then. Let's play."

A Poké Ball detached from Sabrina's belt and began to fly through the air on its own.

"She's controlling the ball with telekinesis!" Brock said. "She can move things with her mind."

Sabrina was focused on the Poké Ball. "Come out, Abra," she said.

There was a flash of light, and then a golden-brown Pokémon appeared on the gym floor. Ash thought Abra looked sort of like a fox. It had a pointy snout, long tail, and big feet.

"Go get it, Pikachu!" Ash commanded.

Pikachu ran up to Abra. It bounced around the Pokémon, looking for a chance to attack. But Abra just sat slumped on the floor. It was sleeping!

"*Pika?*" Pikachu asked.

"I don't get it, either," Ash said. He pulled out Dexter, his Pokédex. Dexter was a tiny computer that held information about all of the world's Pokémon.

Dexter spoke, "Abra. A Psychic Pokémon. It sleeps eighteen hours a day, but uses telekinesis, even while sleeping."

"A sleeping Pokémon!" Ash grinned. "This is going to be easy. Pikachu, Thundershock!"

Pikachu concentrated all of its energy on Abra. Its body glowed with electric heat. With a mighty push, Pikachu aimed an electric shock at Abra.

Sabrina's eyes began to glow red. Abra's eyes slowly opened and glowed red, too.

Pikachu's electric shock flew toward Abra. Just before it hit, the Psychic Pokémon disappeared. Then it reappeared in another spot in the gym.

"It teleported itself!" Ash cried.

Sabrina glared at them. "Childish fools."

"Ash, watch out!" Misty cried. "Something's happening to Abra!"

Ash spun around. Abra was surrounded by a blast of white light.

The light faded. Ash blinked. He looked at Abra.

Abra had changed. It was taller. It had long whiskers and a red star on its forehead.

"What's that?" Ash asked.

"Kadabra," said Dexter. "The evolved form of Abra. Employs powerful telekinetic attacks."

"Be careful!" Misty called out. "That Kadabra is really powerful."

Ash stood firm. "Don't worry. Kadabra won't be able to teleport away from *this* attack." He turned to Pikachu. "Pikachu! Fill up this whole stadium with lightning!"

Pikachu clenched its tiny paws. Small sparks flew from its ears.

"Piiiiiiiiiiika!"

With a mighty cry, Pikachu sent four lightning bolts flying into the air. The lightning bolts whirled around in a circle.

"All right!" Ash knew there was no way for Kadabra to escape.

Sabrina was calm. "Kadabra, confusion!"

Kadabra pointed at the lightning bolts. The bolts began to move as if they were under Kadabra's command. The bolts formed the shape of a terrifying monster — a monster with huge jaws.

Kadabra pointed again. The lightning

monster flew after Pikachu. It opened its jaws wide.

Pikachu was hit with its own electric attack!

The lightning Pokémon collapsed onto the floor. Pikachu slowly got up. It was down, but not out.

"Psychic Attack," commanded Sabrina.

Now Kadabra pointed again. Pikachu began to move its arms and legs.

"Pikachu, stop dancing!" Ash called out. *Why would Pikachu be dancing now?* Ash wondered.

"That's no dance," Misty explained. "Kadabra's using its psychic powers to control Pikachu's body."

Kadabra pointed at the ceiling. With a jolt, Pikachu flew up. *Crash!* Pikachu banged into the ceiling.

Kadabra pointed down. Pikachu went spiraling down. *Crash!* Pikachu slammed onto the gym floor.

Ash cringed. There was no way to fight this Psychic Attack.

Kadabra pointed up again.

Ash ran to the floor and grabbed Pikachu.

"That's it!" Ash said. "I forfeit the match. It's not worth seeing Pikachu get hurt."

Sabrina stepped down from the platform. Her eyes began to glow red.

"Uh, I guess we'll be leaving now," Ash said. He held Pikachu tightly and began to back out of the gym.

"It's not that simple," Sabrina said.

She stared at Ash with her red eyes. "You lost," she said, "and now you can never leave."

3

The Road to Lavender Town

Ash spun around and ran across the gym floor. Misty and Brock were right behind him. They were almost through the open gym door.

Slam! The door flew shut.

"Sabrina used telekinesis to shut the door!" Brock cried.

Misty pounded on the door. "We're trapped!"

Sabrina's red eyes glared at them. In front of her, a man appeared out of nowhere.

The man grabbed Ash, Misty, and Brock.

"Hold on tight!" he said.

Ash felt that familiar tingle. In a split second, they were all teleported out of the gym. They reappeared outside on the street.

Ash looked up at the man. He had a scruffy beard. He wore a blue jacket, and had a cap pulled down low over his face.

"You teleported us out of there!" Ash said. "Why'd you help us?"

"That's not important," the man said gruffly. "What's important is that you're safe now. You should leave Saffron City before it's too late."

The man turned and began to walk away.

Ash rushed after him. "Wait!" he grabbed the man's sleeve.

"What is it?" the man asked.

"I can't leave Saffron City without getting a Marsh Badge," Ash said. "You teleported us. You can tell me how to use telekinesis to beat Sabrina."

The man's eyes began to glow red. Ash

felt his arms and legs begin to move. But *he* wasn't moving them. *The man* was moving them! The man made Ash fly through the air.

"See? You're powerless against telekinesis," the man growled. "You have to be born with these powers. You can't just learn them."

The red glow stopped. Ash could move his arms and legs again. The man turned and walked down the road.

Ash ran after him again. "There's got to be some way!" Ash shouted, "Please! You've got to help me!"

The man sighed. "You don't give up, do you?" He paused. "There is one way. If you capture a Ghost Pokémon from Lavender Town, you *might* have a chance to defeat Sabrina!"

Ash grinned. "All right! I knew there was a way!"

The man shook his head. "What a foolish young man. No one has ever captured a Ghost Pokémon from the haunted Pokémon Tower."

"Haunted tower? What do you —" Ash started to ask, but before he could finish, the man disappeared.

"That was weird," Mindy said. "I sure am ready to leave this place."

"Great!" Ash said. "Cause we'd better head out for Lavender Town right away. It'll be dark in a few hours."

"Ash, are you crazy?" Misty asked. "You heard what he said about the haunted tower."

But Ash didn't pay attention. He was already running toward the gates of Saffron City.

Misty shook her head. "I guess we'd better follow him again."

"You're right," Brock agreed. "But I've got a strange feeling about this."

Hours later, Ash, Pikachu, Misty, and Brock were walking through the woods on the road to Lavender Town. A full moon was starting to rise over the trees. A thick gray fog surrounded them.

Brock led the way with a flashlight.

"Are we there yet?" Ash asked. "I can't wait to catch a Ghost Pokémon. Then I'll beat Sabrina in no time."

"Ash, catching a Ghost Pokémon isn't easy," Brock reminded him.

"Don't forget about the haunted tower," Misty added.

Ash laughed. "I'm not afraid of any —"

Ash stopped in his tracks. The trees parted in front of them. A round stone tower rose up into the night sky. Mist swirled around the tower's pointy roof. The doorway looked like a giant mouth with two eyes above it.

"So Ash," Misty said. "Are you ready to enter the haunted tower?"

4

Welcome to the Tower

From inside Pokémon Tower, Team Rocket looked out the window at Ash and his friends.

"There they are," Jessie said.

"We'll trap them in the tower," James said. "And then we'll capture Pikachu!"

James walked along the creaky wooden floor. "This is going to be so — aaaaah!"

The floorboards beneath James splintered. He crashed through the floor.

Meowth ran to the hole in the floor and

looked down. "He's all right. The floor broke his fall."

Jessie sighed. "Let's go get him."

Meowth stopped her. "L-l-l-ook behind you!" it said, its teeth chattering.

Jessie turned around. Then she let out a piercing scream.

"Run!" she cried.

Jessie grabbed Meowth. The two of them sped across the room.

And fell through the hole in the floor!

Eeeeeeeeeeeek! A shriek filled the night air.

"What was that?" Ash asked.

"It came from inside the tower," Brock said.

"*Pika?*" Pikachu shivered.

"Well, good luck Ash," Misty said. She gave him a small push forward.

Ash turned around. "Hey! You guys have to come with me."

"Okay," Misty said. "But you go in first!"

"No problem," Ash said bravely. He walked up to the wooden door.

Creak! The door opened on its own.

Ash stepped into the tower. Moonlight streamed through the window and lit up the room.

Old, dust-covered furniture filled the room. A chandelier hung from the ceiling.

"This place is creepy," Misty said. "Maybe we should come back when it's daylight."

"Ghosts don't come out during the day," said Ash. "We've got to stay so we can capture a Ghost Pokémon."

"Well, I don't see any here," Brock said. "Let's try the next room."

Brock led them all through a doorway into the next room. Heavy drapes covered the windows. This room was pitch-black.

"Hey, Ghost Pokémon," Brock called out. "If you're in here, say hello!"

Suddenly, the room was filled with light. Candles flickered all around.

"Who — who did that?" Misty wondered.

"I'm not sure," Brock's voice was shaky.

Ash stepped further into the room. "It doesn't matter who," he said. "Look at this stuff!"

There was a long table in the middle of

the room. The table was covered with plates filled with all kinds of delicious food.

"It looks like a party," Misty said.

"Yeah," Brock agreed. "But who's it for?"

A round ball hung from the ceiling. A string dangled down from the ball. Ash grabbed the string. "Check this out. There's a card attached. It says, 'Pull This.'" Ash yanked on the string.

"Ash, no!" Misty cried.

The ball broke open. Ribbons and confetti poured out on top of Ash, Misty, Brock, and Pikachu. A long banner unrolled in front of them.

"'WELCOME,'" Ash read. "But who's welcoming us?"

At Ash's words, a cold wind swept through the room. The plates of food flew off the table. The wind picked up the chairs in the room. They danced wildly in the air.

"Whoa!" Ash felt himself being lifted into the air. He went flying through the room, dodging plates and turkey legs and apples. Ash tried to stop but he couldn't. Around him, Pikachu, Misty, and Brock flew around like they were in a tornado.

"Help!" Ash cried.

As suddenly as the wind started, it stopped. Ash and the others crashed to the ground.

"Let's get out of here!" Ash cried.

5

The Ghost Pokémon

"There's no way I'm going back inside that tower!" Misty cried.

"Me neither!" Brock agreed.

Ash, Misty, Brock, and Pikachu stood in the courtyard outside the tower. Ash looked up at the spooky stone building.

"We've got to go back," Ash said. "It's the only way to capture a Ghost Pokémon. Right, Pikachu?"

"*Pi?*" Pikachu grabbed Ash's ankle and hid its face.

Ash knelt beside the Electric Pokémon.

"Come on, Pikachu. Don't you want to beat Sabrina as badly as I do?"

Pikachu looked thoughtful. Then it nodded its head.

"*Pika!*" it said in a brave voice.

"Then let's go!" Ash said.

He ran ahead. Misty and Brock didn't move.

"Have a nice time!" Misty said nervously.

"We'll both be waiting for you right here," Brock added.

Ash shrugged. "That's fine. Pikachu and I can do this."

Ash walked through the door to Pokémon Tower.

"Hello everybody!" Ash called out. "We're back! Why don't you come out and show us who you are?"

The room was quiet. Then a form began to suddenly appear in front of them.

A purple Pokémon floated in the air! The Pokémon looked like a giant head, with bulging eyes and a wide mouth. Two large, clawed hands floated in the air in front of it.

For a second, Ash was too stunned to move. He slowly reached for his Pokédex. "What is it?" he asked in a hoarse whisper.

"Haunter. A Ghost Pokémon. No further information available," Dexter said.

Haunter stared at Ash with its big eyes. It cackled.

"We can do this," Ash said. "Pikachu, Thundershock!"

Pikachu stepped beside Ash. It concentrated on Haunter. Small sparks began to fly from its body.

But before Pikachu could attack, Haunter vanished!

"Huh?" Ash asked.

Ash felt a tap on his shoulder.

"Not now, Pikachu," Ash said. "We've got to find Haunter."

Ash whirled around. It wasn't Pikachu at all. It was Haunter!

The Ghost Pokémon was inches from Ash's face. It stuck out its long, pink tongue. Its eyeballs popped out of its head.

Ash jumped back. Then he composed himself. "I'm not afraid of you," he said. "Just wait until I capture you!"

Ash reached for a Poké Ball at his belt, then stopped. Something was coming up through the floor.

It was two *more* Pokémon! They were floating through the floor like it wasn't there. One Pokémon was a round, black ball with two eyes and a wide mouth. A cloud of gas surrounded it. The other Pokémon was purple like the first, but it had pointy ears, arms, and legs.

Ash pulled out Dexter. "Better find out about these guys!"

"Gastly. A Ghost Pokémon. Gengar. The evolved form of Gastly," Dexter reported. "No further information available."

"But how am I supposed to catch them?" Ash wailed.

Haunter, Gastly, and Gengar were cackling as though they thought Ash was very funny.

Gengar grabbed a rolled-up newspaper. It thumped Ash on the head.

"Hey!" Ash cried. "Cut it out!"

"Gengar. Gengar." The Ghost Pokémon laughed and laughed. Haunter and Gastly joined in.

Ash couldn't believe it. "Are you guys trying to be funny?" he asked. "Well, I don't think there's anything funny about it."

"Gengar?" Now large tears rolled from Gengar's eyes.

"Haaaauuuuunter," the Ghost Pokémon sobbed.

The three Pokémon began to sink back into the floor.

"Hey! Don't go! I've got to capture you!"
Ash leaped into the air. The Ghost Pokémon
sank into the floor and disappeared. Ash
slammed into the floor.

Pikachu ran to Ash's side. The
vibrations from Ash's collision sent the
chandelier rocking above them. It fell from
the ceiling and landed on Ash and Pikachu.

Ash blacked out. Then he slowly opened
his eyes.

Haunter, Gastly, and Gengar were floating in the air next to them. Ash felt funny — like he was floating, too.

Puzzled, Ash looked down. He saw Pikachu lying on the ground. He saw another body lying on the ground, too.

It was *his* body!

"What's happening?" Ash asked, panicked. He looked at his arms. He could see *right through them*! He looked to his side. Pikachu was floating in the air, too. It was see-through, too.

"Haunter! Haunter, haunter, haunter," the Ghost Pokémon explained.

"Oh, no," Ash moaned as he realized what had

happened. "We've been totally separated from our bodies!"

Haunter grabbed Ash's arm and pulled him through the air.

"But I don't want to be a ghost yet!" Ash yelled frantically.

6

Ash's Ghostly Flight

Haunter pulled Ash up through the ceiling. They passed through it as if it wasn't there.

Ash looked behind him. Pikachu was riding on Gengar's head.

Soon they were outside. The buildings of Lavender Town sparkled below them.

"Wow, what a view," Ash remarked. He wasn't scared anymore.

"*Pika,*" Pikachu agreed.

Ash let go of Haunter's hand. Pikachu floated next to him. Ash spread his arms out wide. He began to fly through the night sky.

"Hey, this is fun!" Ash exclaimed.

The Ghost Pokémon followed as Ash and Pikachu flew over the buildings and into the woods.

"Let's show Misty and Brock!" Ash said.

Ash flew back to the courtyard. His friends were staring at the tower with worried looks on their faces.

"I hope Ash is all right in there," Misty was saying. "We should go check on him."

Ash floated in front of Misty's face. "Hey, I didn't know you cared," he said.

Misty didn't reply. She stared straight ahead.

"She doesn't see me!" Ash said. *"Cool!"*

Ash flew behind Misty. He lifted her high in the air.

"Help! It's a ghost!" Misty cried.

Ash laughed. He lowered Misty to the ground.

"This is so great," he exclaimed. "What's next?"

Haunter pointed to Pokémon Tower. Ash and Pikachu followed the Ghost Pokémon through a window.

They were in a room filled with toys. Gastly swung on a swing set. Haunter and Gengar went up and down on a seesaw.

"Look at all these toys!" Ash remarked.

"*Haunter, haunter, haunter!*" the Ghost Pokémon repeated.

"I get it," Ash said. "You guys are lonely in this tower all by yourselves. You just want someone to play with."

"*Haunter! Haunter!*" Haunter smiled.

Pikachu hopped up on the swing with Gastly. The Ghost Pokémon all looked so happy.

"I wish I could stay and play with you," Ash said. "But I have to fulfill my dream of becoming a Pokémon Master."

"Haaaaaauunter." All of the Ghost Pokémon began to sob and cry.

"Come on, Pikachu," Ash said. "We'd better go."

Ash and Pikachu floated down through the floor. They came to the first floor. Brock and Misty were kneeling over their bodies. Ash and Pikachu waved good-bye to the Ghost Pokémon and then floated back into their bodies.

Ash opened his eyes. His head hurt. He was back inside his own body again.

Misty smiled with relief. "You're all right!"

"Pika!" Pikachu sat up.

"We're okay," Ash said. "But we should really go now."

The friends walked back into the court-yard.

"But Ash, what about the Ghost Pokémon?" Misty asked.

Ash shook his head. "It's impossible to

catch them." Ash walked away from the tower.

"Haunter!"

Haunter popped up in front of them. It stuck out its tongue and made a scary face.

"Eeeeeeeek!" Misty and Brock screamed.

Ash laughed. "It's okay." he said. "This is Haunter. I think it wants to come with us after all."

"Haunter, haunter!" Haunter nodded.

"Then let's get back to Saffron City!" Ash said.

Meanwhile, inside Pokémon Tower, Gengar and Gastly were having fun with some new friends.

"I can't take anymore!" cried Jessie. Gengar was spinning Team Rocket around on a toy merry-go-round.

"Let me off! I'm dizzy!" James yelled.

Meowth's stomach lurched as the merry-go-round spun around again. "It looks like Team Rocket's throwing up again!"

7

The Battle Begins

Ash and his friends gazed up at the Saffron City Gym.

"It's time to beat Sabrina and earn my Marsh Badge," Ash declared.

Brock backed away. "Good luck, Ash."

"Yeah, give it your best shot," Misty said.

"Aren't you coming in with me?" Ash asked.

Misty and Brock looked at each other.

"Sabrina's dangerous, Ash," Misty said.

"You've got nothing to worry about,"

Ash said. "With Haunter on my side, I'm guaranteed to win that badge!"

"*Haunter!*" The Ghost Pokémon grinned and nodded.

Ash faced his friends. "Are you with me?"

Misty and Brock sighed. Then they nodded.

"Great!" Ash said. "Let's go battle Sabrina."

At Ash's words, the door to the gym opened by itself. Ash and the others stepped on to the gym floor. Sabrina was standing on the platform at the end of the gym. She was holding a Poké Ball.

"Sabrina! I've come back for a rematch!" Ash shouted.

Sabrina's body lifted off the ground. She flew through the air from the platform onto the ground.

"You don't have a chance," she said coldly.

Ash stood firm. "This time you won't have it so easy!"

Sabrina glared at him. "If you lose this time," she said, "there's no escape."

A Poké Ball flew from Sabrina's hands.

"Go Kadabra!" she called out.

The Psychic Pokémon appeared in a blaze of light.

"And I choose Haunter!" Ash said. "Go, Haunter!"

Sabrina's eyes narrowed. "So you captured a Ghost Pokémon, did you?" she said. "Where is it?"

Ash looked around the gym. Haunter was nowhere to be seen.

"Haunter! It's time for the battle!" Ash cried.

There was no reply.

"It looks like the Ghost Pokémon got spooked," Brock remarked.

"Enough stalling!" Sabrina said angrily. "Send out your Pokémon at once!"

Ash turned to Pikachu. "Please, Pikachu?"

Pikachu trembled and shook its head.

Ash was panicked. Without Haunter, there was no way he could beat Sabrina.

"I know what to do," Ash said. "I quit! Run for it, guys!"

Ash grabbed Pikachu and ran for the gym doors. He hoped Sabrina was too surprised to catch up to them.

Ash ran outside into the sunlight.

"Help!" The scream came from inside the gym.

Sabrina's eyes glowed yellow. Beams of light flashed at Misty and Brock as they ran away.

Suddenly, Misty and Brock stopped in their tracks.

"I'm frozen!" Misty cried.

Brock strained to move. "She's frozen us with her psychic powers!"

"No!" Ash cried. He started to run back in.

The door slammed shut in front of him.

Misty and Brock were trapped inside with Sabrina!

8

Team Rocket Returns

"I see your friends are in trouble."

Ash spun around. It was the man with telekinetic powers!

"What can we do?" Ash asked.

"You must defeat Sabrina," the man said. "Didn't you travel to Lavender Town to find a Ghost Pokémon?"

Ash nodded. "I found Haunter. But it's disappeared."

"Then we must find Haunter," the man said. "I'll help you."

Ash, Pikachu, and the man walked the

streets of Saffron City. Tall office buildings rose above them.

"We've got to find Haunter and beat Sabrina," Ash said. "She's the meanest trainer I've ever met!"

"She wasn't always so bad," the man said.

"What do you mean?" Ash asked.

"Sabrina was born with psychic powers," the man explained. "When she was very young, she became obsessed with her powers. She didn't want to make friends. She just wanted to be left alone to develop her telekinesis. Now it's taken control of her. It's like she's in a deep sleep."

Ash kicked at the ground. "I guess that's a pretty sad story. But I still need to defeat her to save Misty and Brock." Ash turned to Pikachu. "Where do you think Haunter could be?"

"Pika, pika." Pikachu didn't know.

"We'll find Haunter," Ash said. "We have to!"

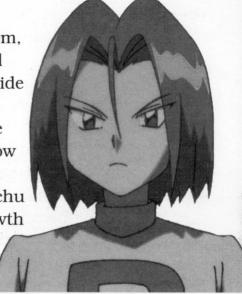

High above them, Team Rocket stood on a platform outside an office building window. They were disguised as window washers.

"*Meowth!* Pikachu will be ours," Meowth said, looking down on Ash and Pikachu. "What secret weapon did you cook up this time?"

"It's a deadly weapon that's been perfected over thousands of years," James said. He pulled out a fishing net.

"*That's* your secret weapon?" Meowth asked.

"Sometimes the simplest weapon is the best weapon," Jessie said. "Just watch."

Jessie and James began to lower the net.

Suddenly, something appeared in front of them.

It was Haunter!

"Haunter!" cried the Ghost Pokémon. It stuck out its tongue.

Startled, Jessie, James, and Meowth jumped back. The force was too much for the flimsy platform. The rope holding up the platform snapped in two.

Jessie, James, and Meowth plummeted to the ground!

"Haunt, haunt!" Laughing, Haunter grabbed the fishing net. The Ghost Pokémon flew to the ground and held open the net. Jessie, James, and Meowth landed safely in it.

Haunter tied up the net. He flew to Ash's side and deposited the Team Rocket bundle at Ash's feet.

"What's this?" Ash asked. Then it hit him. "Haunter! You stopped them from capturing Pikachu!"

Haunter nodded.

"Way to go! Now let's get back to Sabrina's gym," Ash said.

"Haunter?" Haunter didn't sound so excited.

"Please, Haunter," Ash pleaded. "We've

got to help Misty and Brock. Sabrina trapped them inside the gym."

Haunter looked thoughtful. Then it smiled and nodded. *"Haunter!"*

"Thanks, Haunter," Ash said. "Now let's go save my friends!"

9

Haunter vs. Kadabra

"How do we get in?" Ash tried to open the doors to the gym. They were shut tight.

"No problem," the man said. He stared at the doors. His eyes glowed. The doors flew open.

"Cool!" Ash said. "Now let's do this."

Ash and Pikachu stepped onto the gym floor. Haunter floated beside them. Sabrina was seated on the platform. Brock and Misty stood on either side of her. They looked like statues.

"I knew you'd be back," Sabrina said.

"Have you returned for more humiliation? Haven't you realized yet that you'll never defeat me?"

"Brock and Misty are my friends and I can't leave them behind!" Ash said.

"Fine. Let's begin," Sabrina said. A Poké Ball floated in the air in front of her. "I choose Kadabra!"

Kadabra appeared on the gym floor.

"I choose Haunter!" Ash called out.

Haunter was nowhere to be seen.

"Not again!" Ash cried. He yelled into the air. "Haunter! You promised me!"

Sabrina's eyes began to glow yellow. "Perhaps you'd like to join your friends."

Pikachu jumped into the center of the gym floor. It faced Kadabra.

"Pikachu!" Pikachu cried.

Kadabra towered over the small Electric Pokémon.

"Pikachu, come back!" Ash called out. "You don't stand a chance against Kadabra."

Pikachu faced Ash. *"Pika. Pika pika pika pi."*

Ash understood. "You don't want Sabrina to freeze me, too? You want to fight?"

Pikachu nodded.

Ash knew he couldn't stop Pikachu when its mind was made up. He took a deep breath. "Okay, then. Pikachu, Thunder-shock!"

Pikachu hurled a giant blast of thunder at Kadabra.

"Kadabra! Teleport!" Sabrina cried.

Kadabra disappeared. The Thundershock harmlessly hit the gym floor. Then Kadabra appeared in another spot in the gym.

"Kadabra, Psybeam!" Sabrina commanded.

Kadabra faced Pikachu. Rainbow beams shot out of Kadabra's eyes. The beams hit Pikachu and sent it reeling backward.

"Try to hang on, Pikachu!" Ash called out. "Send out a Thunderbolt."

Pikachu's body tensed. It sent a lightning bolt of electricity right into Kadabra's body. Kadabra doubled over. Its body crackled with the electric charge.

"Kadabra, recover!" Sabrina said.

Kadabra straightened up. It shook off the charge like it was nothing.

"Pika!" Pikachu couldn't believe it.

Ash didn't know what to do. If he left Pikachu in the battle, it would only get hurt. If he gave up, he and his friends would be frozen — forever.

"Haunter!"

Ash looked behind him. Haunter floated through the gym doors. The man with telekinetic powers followed it.

Sabrina frowned. "Two against one is against the rules."

"Haunter is playing around on its own," the man called out. "There's no rule against that."

Haunter floated up next to Sabrina. It

put its fingers in its mouth and opened its mouth wide.

Sabrina eyed Haunter curiously.

Haunter spun around and around in the air. It popped its eyeballs out of its head. It stuck its tongue out and licked Sabrina right on the face.

Ash waited for Sabrina to yell. Or freeze Haunter.

But she didn't.

Sabrina smiled!

"Haunt, haunt, haunt, haunt!" Haunter laughed and laughed.

Now Sabrina was laughing, too.

"I can't believe it!" Ash said. "Haunter was supposed to beat Sabrina. Now he's making her laugh! I'll never win this match."

The man smiled. "Look over there."

Ash looked out on the gym floor. Kadabra was doubled over with laughter.

"Kadabra and Sabrina are joined tele-pathically," the man explained. "Whatever she feels, Kadabra feels."

The man yelled loudly, "Since Kadabra

is no longer able to battle, I declare Pikachu the winner! Ash earns his Marsh Badge." A small round badge appeared in the man's hand. He gave it to Ash.

"All right!" Ash said. "But what about —"

"Ash!" Misty cried. She ran down from the platform. She wasn't frozen anymore.

"You did it!" It was Brock. He was back to normal, too.

Ash hugged his friends. "I'm glad you're okay. It's all thanks to —"

Ash turned to thank the mysterious man. He was hugging Sabrina. Sabrina's eyes looked bright and clear — as if she had just woken up from a long sleep.

"I get it," Ash said. "When Haunter made Sabrina laugh, it was like he broke a spell. Her psychic powers aren't controlling her anymore."

Sabrina smiled at the man. "Dad," she said. "Is it really you?"

"It's me, Sabrina," the man said. "I missed you so much."

"Wow!" Ash said. "So that man was Sabrina's father all along."

"That's pretty amazing," Misty said. "And so is your Marsh Badge, Ash. Congratulations!"

"Thanks," Ash said. He looked at the badge in his hand. "Are you sure I deserve it?"

"Sure," Misty said. "Making Sabrina laugh is a great strategy."

"Hmmm," Ash said. "Maybe I'll use humor to win my next badge!"

"Keep it up and you'll be known as the funniest Pokémon Master of all time!" Brock teased.

"Then let's get going," Ash said. "I've got more badges to win."

So Ash and his friends left the Saffron City Gym — ready to begin their next adventure!

About the Author

Tracey West has been writing books for more than ten years. When she's not playing the blue version of the Pokémon game (she started with a Squirtle), she enjoys reading comic books, watching cartoons, and taking long walks in the woods (looking for wild Pokémon). She lives in a small town in New York with her family and pets.

Coming Soon . . . .

Pokémon The Movie
Mewtwo Strikes Back!

Novelization based on the new movie

Mewtwo, the super Pokémon, is trying to take over the world! It's the biggest Pokémon battle ever! Only the legendary Pokémon, Mew, can save the world from Mewtwo's super strength.

Pikachu's Vacation

Junior novelization based on the cartoon shown with *Mewtwo Strikes Back!*

Pikachu and its Pokémon friends are having a fun-filled day at the Pokémon playground. Until . . . *uh-oh!* A group of bullies show up. Now it's a Pokémon battle to be master of the playground.

Catch 'em in November!